Big Bear
Little Bear

DAVID BEDFORD AND JANE CHAPMAN

LITTLE TIGER PRESS

One bright cold morning, Little Bear
helped Mama Bear scoop snow out
of their den.

"This will make more room for you
to play," said Mama Bear. "You are
getting bigger now."

"I want to be as big as you when I'm
grown-up," said Little Bear. He stretched
up his arms and made himself as big
as he could.

Mama Bear stretched to the sky.
"You'll have to eat and eat to be
as big as I am," she said.
"When I'm big, I'll wrestle you in
the snow," said Little Bear. Wrestling
in the snow was his favorite game.

"You're not big enough to wrestle me yet," said Mama Bear, laughing.

She rolled Little Bear over and over in the soft snow and he giggled.

"When I'm grown-up I want to run as fast as you, Mommy," he said.

"You'll have to practice if you want to be as fast as I am," said Mama Bear.

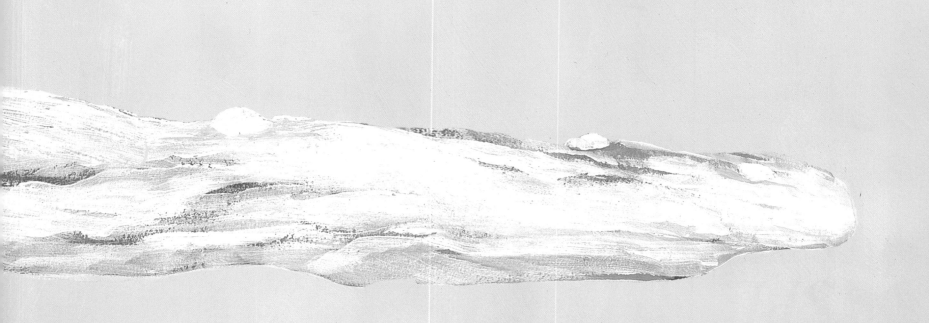

Little Bear darted away and
ran as fast as he could . . .

but Mama Bear quickly passed him, calling, "Run faster!"

"I can't," said Little Bear. "I'm not grown-up yet."

"I'll show you what it's like to be grown-up," said Mama Bear. "Climb onto my shoulders!"

When Little Bear stood on his mother's shoulders he could see to the end of the world and when he reached up his hands he could almost touch the sky.

"Now you *are* big," said Mama Bear.

"Let's run," cried Mama Bear. She ran
faster and faster, so that Little Bear felt
the wind rushing against his face and
blowing his ears back.

Suddenly, Mama Bear leapt into the air.
Little Bear saw the world rushing under him.
"I'm flying like a bird," he shouted. Then
he saw where they were going to land . . .

...SPLASH!

Mama Bear dove into the cold water. "This is how you'll swim when you're grown-up," she said.

Little Bear watched his mother carefully so he would know what to do next time.

"I'll soon be able to swim like that," he told himself.

Mama Bear climbed out of the water with Little Bear still clinging tightly to her back.

"Will I *really* be as big as you when I'm grown-up?" asked Little Bear.

"Yes, you will," said his mother, "but I don't want you to grow up yet."

"Why not?" asked Little Bear.

"You won't be able to sit on my
shoulders when you're grown-up,"
said Mama Bear, as she carried
Little Bear back to their snow den.

Little Bear was tired after wrestling,
running, flying, and swimming.
   "You can still cuddle me when I'm
grown-up," he said, sleepily. "But Mommy,
I don't want to grow up yet."

"That's good," said Mama Bear,
holding him close, "because . . .